THERE'S A LION in My CORNFLAKES

Michelle Robinson illustrated by Jim Field

BLOOMSBURY
NEW YORK LONDON NEW DELHI SYDNEY

If you ever see this on a box of cornflakes:

ignore it!
JUICE
MILK
I'll tell you what happened when we didn't . . .

My brother, Dan, and I made a million trips to the supermarket and spent a whole year's allowance on cereal.

It took us a LONG time to cut out all the coupons.

Mom was so mad she made us eat cornflakes for breakfast, lunch, and dinner.

She said we'd have nothing but cornflakes
until they were all gone.

That could take forever!

And she said we wouldn't get any allowance until we'd eaten up every last boring, crunchy flake.

But we didn't mind. We really wanted a free lion.

We could take it for walks.

Ride it to school.

And use it to open tin cans.*

But everyone else had the same idea.

We waited and waited for our free lion to arrive.
But there was no lion on Monday . . . or Tuesday . . . or Wednesday.

Thursday? No lion.

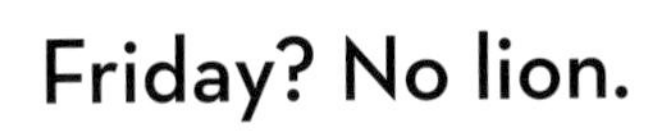

Friday? No lion.

Saturday? STILL no lion.

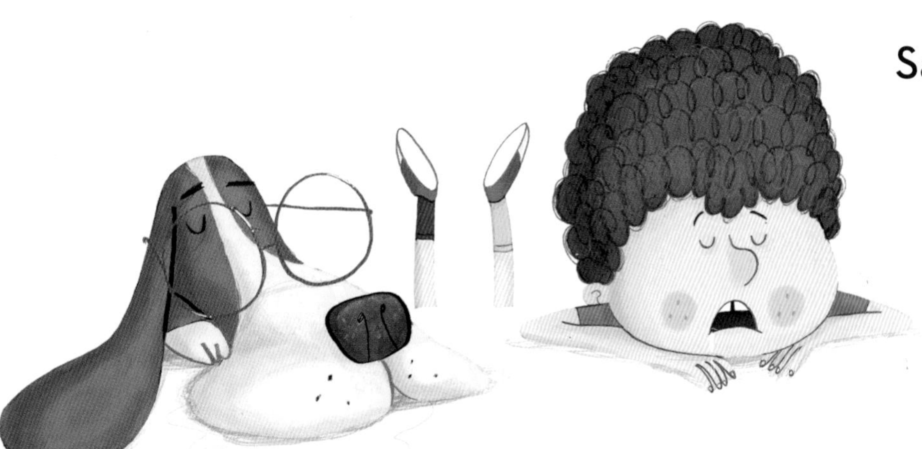

Even worse, by the time Sunday came . . .

Enjoy a
MR. WHIPPY

EVERYONE else had theirs. How unfair is that?!

Then on Monday, a delivery truck arrived.
We were so excited!

But, one: it wasn't a lion.
Two: they sent it next door by mistake.
And three: it went crazy in Mr. Harper's backyard.

It wasn't our fault! But Mom went bonkers.
She made us apologize to Mr. Harper AND clean up.
It was awful. We had a grizzly bear, a grumpy mom,
and absolutely NO free lion.

We wrote to the cereal people and complained.
They wrote back:

Mr. Flaky
LTD

Dan and Eric
Pink House
Hilly Hill
Bookland

Dear Eric and Dan,

Sorry about the grizzly bear, but we ran out of lions.

Please accept this crocodile instead.

Sincerely,

Mr. Flaky

Mr. Flaky

P.S. Handle with care.

“A crocodile?!” Dan said. “We didn’t eat all those cornflakes for a cranky old crocodile!”

And guess what? The crocodile spent all its time in the bathroom, so no one else could get in.

Dad went nuts. He made us scrub the bathtub while he called the cereal people. "Sorry," they said. "We'll sort it out right away."

We asked for a LION.
NOT a grizzly bear, NOT a bathroom-hogging crocodile, and . . .

. . . DEFINITELY not a great big gorilla. But that's exactly what we got.
It really liked Dad's car.

He was not impressed.
"That's it," he fumed. "Everyone in—I'm going to give those cereal people a piece of my mind!"

The cereal people said sorry—AGAIN—but they really had run out of lions.
They said that we could keep the great big gorilla, the bathroom-hogging crocodile, and the very grizzly bear.
They also gave us . . .

. . . a lifetime's supply of cornflakes.
Finally, Dad was happy. But Mom wasn't—and we certainly weren't.

You can't take a box of cornflakes for a walk.

Cornflakes won't get you to school in style.

Can cornflakes help you open a can of tomatoes? No way!

But . . .

A crocodile is the meanest can-opening machine I've ever seen!

A grizzly bear can walk for miles and miles . . . and miles!

And there isn't a better way to
arrive at school than this!

So don't ever bother saving up for a lion;
it's not worth the trouble.
And besides, EVERYONE'S got one.

But a free tiger? Just imagine . . .

Mr. Flaky
CORN FLAKES
CORN FLAKES
NUTRITION FACTS
FREE TIGER
JUST SAVE 100 COUPONS
MILK

For my brother, Dan —M. R.
For Sandy —J. F.

First published in Great Britain in July 2014 by Bloomsbury Publishing Plc
Published in the United States of America in May 2015 by Bloomsbury Children's Books
www.bloomsbury.com

Bloomsbury is a registered trademark of Bloomsbury Publishing Plc

For information about permission to reproduce selections from this book, write to
Permissions, Bloomsbury Children's Books, 1385 Broadway, New York, New York 10018
Bloomsbury books may be purchased for business or promotional use. For information on bulk purchases please contact
Macmillan Corporate and Premium Sales Department at specialmarkets@macmillan.com

Library of Congress Cataloging-in-Publication Data
Robinson, Michelle (Michelle Jane).
There's a lion in my cornflakes / by Michelle Robinson ; illustrated by Jim Field.
pages cm
Summary: If you ever see a box of cornflakes offering a free lion, ignore it. This is the story of two brothers who didn't—and then ended up with a grizzly bear, a cranky old crocodile, and a huge gorilla instead.
ISBN 978-0-8027-3836-3 (hardcover) • ISBN 978-1-61963-697-2 (e-book) • ISBN 978-1-61963-698-9 (e-PDF)
[1. Cereals, Prepared—Fiction. 2. Animals—Fiction. 3. Humorous stories.] I. Field, Jim, illustrator. II. Title. III. Title: There is a lion in my cornflakes.
PZ7.R567535Th 2015 [E]—dc23 2014020004

Art created digitally • Typeset in Neutraface • Book design by Zoe Waring

Printed in China by Leo Paper Products, Heshan, Guangdong
2 4 6 8 10 9 7 5 3 1

All papers used by Bloomsbury Publishing, Inc., are natural, recyclable products made from wood grown in well-managed forests.
The manufacturing processes conform to the environmental regulations of the country of origin.